Usborne Farmyard Tales

Surprise Visitors

Heather Amery

Illustrated by Stephen Cartwright

Language consultant: Betty Root
Series editor: Jenny Tyler

There is a little yellow duck to find on every page.

This is Apple Tree Farm.

This is Mrs. Boot, the farmer. She has two children, called Poppy and Sam, and a dog called Rusty.

Today is Saturday.

Mrs. Boot, Poppy and Sam are having breakfast.
"Why are the cows so noisy?" asks Sam.

They all run out to the field.

The cows are running around the field. They are scared. A big balloon is floating over the trees.

"It's a hot air balloon."

"It's coming down," says Mrs. Boot. "It's going to land in our field." The balloon hits the ground.

There are two people in it.

"Where are we?" asks the man. "This is Apple Tree Farm. You frightened our cows," says Mrs. Boot.

The man climbs out.

"I'm Alice and this is Tim," says the woman.
"We ran out of gas. Sorry about your cows."

"A truck is following us."

"There it is now," says Alice. "Our friend is bringing more cylinders of gas for the balloon."

Alice helps to unload the truck.

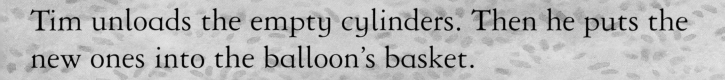

Tim unloads the empty cylinders. Then he puts the new ones into the balloon's basket.

They blow up the balloon.

Poppy and Sam help Tim hold open the balloon.
A fan blows hot air into it. It gets bigger and bigger.

"Would you like a ride?"

"Oh, yes please," says Poppy. "Just a little one,"
says Tim. "The truck will bring you back."

Mrs. Boot, Poppy and Sam climb in.

Tim lights the gas burner. The big flames make a loud noise. "Hold on tight," says Alice.

The balloon goes up.

Slowly it leaves the ground. Tim turns off the burner. "The wind is blowing us along," he says.

The balloon floats along.

"I can see our farm down there," says Poppy.
"Look, there's Alice in the truck," says Sam.

"We're going down now," says Tim.

The balloon floats down and the basket lands in a field. Mrs. Boot helps Poppy and Sam out.

"Thank you very much."

They wave as the balloon takes off again.
"We were flying," says Sam.

Cover design by Hannah Ahmed   Digital manipulation by Sarah Cronin